E
AB

Abolafia, Yossi

My three uncles

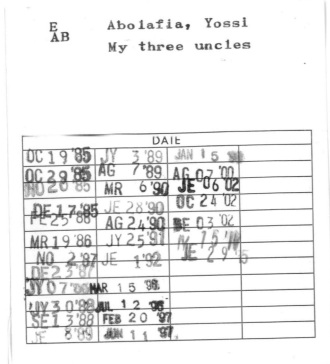

DATE			
OC 19 '85	JY 3 '89	JAN 15	
OC 29 '85	AG 7 '89	AG 07 '00	
NO 28 '85	MR 6 '90	JE 06 02	
DE 17 '85	JE 28 '90	OC 24 '02	
FE 25 '86	AG 24 '90	SE 03 '02	
MR 19 '86	JY 25 '91	NO 15 '14	
NO 2 '87	JE 1 '92	JE 29 '15	
DE 23 '87			
JY 07 '00	MAR 15 '96		
JY 30 '88	JUL 12 '96		
SE 13 '88	FEB 20 '97		
JE 8 '89	JUN 11 '97		

© THE BAKER & TAYLOR CO.

YOSSI ABOLAFIA

MY THREE UNCLES

Greenwillow Books, New York

FOR MY FATHER

Library of Congress Cataloging in Publication Data
Abolafia, Yossi.   My three uncles.
Summary: A young girl learns how to tell
her three look-alike uncles apart.
[1. Triplets—Fiction.   2. Uncles—Fiction]   I. Title.
PZ7.A165My   1984   [E]   84-4195
ISBN 0-688-04024-1   ISBN 0-688-04025-X (lib. bdg.)

My three uncles are triplets. They look
so much alike people can't tell them apart.
Even I have trouble knowing who is who.

Uncle Jeff is an airline pilot.

Uncle Max is an artist.

Uncle Gilbert works in a bank.

One morning in the zoo, a lady thought Uncle Jeff was Uncle Max.

"That does it," Uncle Jeff said. "I'm tired of being mistaken
  for you two. I'm going to grow a mustache."
"Good," Uncle Max said. "I'll grow a mustache and a beard."
"Then I'll stay the way I am," Uncle Gilbert said.
  Great, I thought. It will be easy to tell them apart.

On my birthday they all came to dinner.

"Hello, Uncle Gilbert," I greeted the first one to arrive.

"I'm not Gilbert," he said, "I'm Jeff."

"But didn't you say you would grow a mustache?"

"I did," said Jeff, "but it tickled so I shaved it off."

Then there was a knock at the door.
"Same old Gilbert, never rings the
bell," my mother said. "Let him in."

"Gilbert?" I asked. He nodded.
"You've changed."
"No I haven't," said Gilbert.
"I just grew a mustache."

Suddenly there was a loud thump.

"It's only Max," my mother said.

"He's coming through the kitchen window again. Always playing tricks."

"We do have a front door, you know," she said.

"I know," said Max.
"But there are
two animals blocking
the way."

I went to the front door to
check. There were two hamsters
in a box—my birthday present
from Uncle Max.

Uncle Jeff brought me a Walkman
and Uncle Gilbert a piggy bank.
I gave them party hats.

"How can I tell you apart," I asked Uncle Max,
"when you keep changing all the time?"
"Easy," he said. "Just watch us very closely
and you'll see how different we are."

I watched my uncles carefully
all through dinner.
Uncle Gilbert was very serious.
When he spoke he sounded like
the news on TV.

Uncle Jeff wiped his clean fork
with his napkin before he started
eating. He only ate the vegetables.
He wouldn't even touch dessert.
"Too sweet," he said.

Uncle Max wouldn't stop clowning.
He tucked a napkin into his
collar and slurped his soup.
"Stop it, Max," my mother said.
"You are teaching the child
bad manners."

We all helped clean up after dinner, except for Uncle Jeff. He was doing push-ups. "He's always exercising," Uncle Max said, "especially when there is cleaning up to do."

A few weeks later we all met at the beach. I couldn't believe it. My three uncles all had mustaches. I began to think maybe they did it on purpose just to confuse me. But I knew right away which one was Max. Who else would make a snowman in the middle of July?

"Hello, Uncle Max!" I called. "See, I recognized you right away."
"Very good," said Uncle Max. "But how about Jeff and Gilbert?"

"That's easy. The one with the sunglasses is . . ."
I was about to say Uncle Jeff, but then
I thought, No, Uncle Jeff is always moving.
So I said, "It's Uncle Gilbert."
"Wrong," said Max. "It's Jeff.
Too much exercise."

Uncle Jeff jumped up. "Got to keep in shape," he said.

Uncle Gilbert hardly moved all day.

On Halloween night we gave a party. I watched the guests arriving: a ghost, a witch, and a rabbit. They weren't my uncles.

A bee was getting out of a taxi. I stood behind the door
and waited. There was a knock, then another knock.

"Hi, Uncle Gilbert," I said, opening the door.

"You recognized me?" said Gilbert, surprised.

"You haven't changed," I said.

"You never ring the bell."

I was sure the next person
who came was Uncle Jeff.

He waved to my mother and
walked straight to the food.
He examined the cold cuts
and sniffed the meatballs.

That can't be Uncle Jeff, I thought.
He smiled at me.

He took a plate and piled
it high with green salad.
It's Uncle Jeff!
He took a big mouthful.

"Hello, Uncle Max," I said.
"Max?" he laughed. "You mean Jeff."
"Come on, Uncle Max," I said.
"You can't fool me anymore."

"How did you know?" asked Max.

"Uncle Jeff would never use a fork
without wiping it first," I said.

"Really," said Max.

"I guess I should
watch more carefully."

I went to look for Uncle Jeff.

He can't be the clown. He's too tall.
Maybe the one with the lampshade over his head?
No, that's my father.
I went back to Uncle Max.

"Uncle Max," I said, "I can't find Uncle Jeff.
I don't think he is here."

Max lifted me up and threw me in the air.
"I knew you'd figure it out!" he said.
"Jeff couldn't come. He had to fly to
Singapore. But he left a surprise for
you. It's under your pillow."

I ran up to my room.
I can finally tell my uncles apart,
I thought.

I opened the box. . . .

Now I even look like them.